Respecting the Contributions of
African Americans

Anna Kingston

PowerKiDS
press

New York

Published in 2013 by The Rosen Publishing Group, Inc.
29 East 21st Street, New York, NY 10010

First Edition

Editor: Jennifer Way
Book Design: Erica Clendening and Ashley Drago
Layout Design: Andrew Povolny

Photo Credits: Cover Patrick Smith/Getty Images; p. 5 Inti St. Clair/Photodisc/Getty Images; p. 6 Jupiterimages/ Brand X Pictures/Getty Images; p. 7 © iStockphoto.com/Images by Barbara; p. 8 Photo Researchers/Getty Images; p. 9 MPI/Archive Photos/Getty Images; p. 11 Russell Lee/Archive Photos/Getty Images; p. 12 Kevork Djansezian/ Getty Images; p. 13 Keystone/Hulton Archive/Getty Images; p. 14 Frank Driggs Collection/Archive Photos/Getty Images; p. 15 Fred Stein Archive/Archive Photos/Getty Images; pp. 16, 21 Francis Miller/Time & Life Pictures/Getty Images; p. 17 Bachrach/Archive Photos/Getty Images; pp. 19, 20 Don Cravens/Time & Life Images/Getty Images; p. 22 Ciaran Griffin/Stockbyte/Getty Images.

Library of Congress Cataloging-in-Publication Data

Kingston, Anna.
 Respecting the contributions of African Americans / by Anna Kingston. — 1st ed.
    p. cm. — (Stop bullying now!)
 Includes index.
 ISBN 978-1-4488-7448-4 (library binding) — ISBN 978-1-4488-7521-4 (pbk.) —
 ISBN 978-1-4488-7595-5 (6-pack)
 1. African Americans—History—Juvenile literature. 2. African Americans—Civil rights—History—Juvenile literature.
 3. United States—Civilization—African American influences—Juvenile literature. I. Title.
 E185.K47 2013
 973'.0496073—dc23
                                        2012005643

Manufactured in the United States of America

CPSIA Compliance Information: Batch #SW12PK: For Further Information contact Rosen Publishing, New York, New York at 1-800-237-9932

Contents

How many famous African Americans can you name? Your list is likely long. African Americans, or Americans whose families have roots in Africa, have found success in many fields. Some, such as Patricia Bath and George Washington Carver, became inventors. Others, such as Faith Ringgold and Toni Morrison, are writers. President Barack Obama is an African American, as are the singer Jay-Z and the football star Adrian Peterson.

African Americans have played a central role in American history from its start. However, their struggle to be treated fairly has been long and hard. In fact, that struggle continues today.

Some African American families celebrate Kwanzaa. This weeklong celebration honors their African roots and focuses on learning about important values.

Dealing with Bullying

African American kids sometimes face bullying. Bullies are people who do things that hurt other people or make them feel threatened. Bullies often pick on kids who are different.

Text bullying is when bullies send hateful texts to someone. About 1 in 5 kids will be text bullied at some point.

Kids who are bullied often feel lonely and afraid. Trusted adults, such as parents or teachers, can help if you or someone at your school is being bullied.

Bullies hurt people in many ways. Some bullies call people bad names or make fun of people for how they look, act, or talk. Bullies who say hurtful things about others online are known as **cyberbullies**.

Making others feel left out is bullying, too. For example, a bully might refuse to be friends with a kid because he is African American. Treating people differently because of their race is **racism**.

The Horrors of Slavery

Most African Americans have **ancestors** who were brought from Africa as slaves hundreds of years ago. Slaves had little control over their own lives. They could be whipped if they disobeyed the person who owned them. Slave families were separated when their masters sold family members.

Most slaves lived in the South, where they worked on big farms, called **plantations**. By the mid-nineteenth century, slavery was against the law in the North. Disagreements over slavery caused the Civil War, which was fought between the North and the South from 1861 until 1865. By the war's end, the North won and slavery ended.

◀ Families of slaves were often broken up and sold to different people. This painting shows a slave market.

Harriet Tubman (1820?-1913)

Harriet Tubman was born a slave in Maryland around 1820. In 1849, she ran away and reached freedom in Philadelphia, Pennsylvania. A year later, she returned to lead her sister and other slaves north to freedom. In all, Tubman returned to the South 19 times to guide escaping slaves.

A Continuing Struggle

In 1865, the Thirteenth **Amendment** was added to the US **Constitution**. It outlawed slavery. In 1868, the Fourteenth and Fifteenth Amendments were added. They said that African Americans were full **citizens** and that African-American men could vote.

However, African Americans were still treated unfairly. In many places, white Americans made it very hard for them to vote. Many states passed laws that kept African Americans from drinking from the same drinking fountains or riding in the same train cars as white people. The separation of African Americans and whites is known as **segregation**.

Segregation lasted from the end of the Civil War until the 1960s. Here a man in Oklahoma in 1939 drinks from a drinking fountain for African Americans.

African Americans faced violence as well as segregation. Between 1880 and 1950, more than 3,000 African Americans were **lynched**, or killed by mobs. Lynch mobs took the law into their own hands. They killed people as punishment and to scare other African Americans.

The NAACP is still active today. Here are members in 2011 marching in support of grocery store workers who want better pay and benefits.

W. E. B. Du Bois formed the NAACP to secure the constitutional and civil rights of African Americans.

In 1909, the National Association for the Advancement of Colored People (NAACP) formed to fight lynching. The group would become key in the fight for African-American rights.

The **scholar** W. E. B. Du Bois helped found the NAACP. His 1903 book, *The Souls of Black Folk*, examined the challenges facing African Americans. He also edited the NAACP's journal, *The Crisis*.

African Americans in the Arts

The Cotton Club was a famous Harlem jazz club. Duke Ellington, Count Basie, Billie Holiday, and Lena Horne are just a few of the great African-American jazz musicians who played there.

The Crisis published works by African-American writers who were involved in the **Harlem Renaissance,** such as Countee Cullen. This movement of artists, writers, thinkers, and others celebrated the role of African Americans in America during the 1920s and early 1930s. It was based in the New York City neighborhood of Harlem and included people from many fields, such as writer Zora Neale Hurston, actor Paul Robeson, and artist Aaron Douglas.

Harlem also became a center for **jazz**, a form of music invented by African Americans in the early twentieth century. Duke Ellington was a leading jazz musician of the Harlem Renaissance.

Langston Hughes (1902–1967)

One of the major poets of the Harlem Renaissance was Langston Hughes. Hughes was born in Joplin, Missouri, in 1902. He was a big fan of jazz. This helped shape his poems, such as "A Dream Deferred." Along with poems, Hughes wrote plays, novels, and short stories.

An End to School Segregation

For the first half of the twentieth century, many American schools were segregated. In 1951, school officials kept third-grader Linda Brown from going to her neighborhood school in Topeka, Kansas, because

Many communities fought school integration. Here troops are protecting an African-American student from white racists as she enters Little Rock Central High School in 1957.

she was African American. Linda's father went to court to change this. The NAACP worked with him, and the case reached the Supreme Court. In 1954, the court decided that school segregation in America had to end.

Some communities ended segregation peacefully. Others fought the decision. For example, troops had to be brought in to protect African-American students at Little Rock Central High School in Little Rock, Arkansas, in 1957.

Thurgood Marshall (1908–1993)

Thurgood Marshall was one of the NAACP lawyers who argued the *Brown v. Board of Education* case in front of the Supreme Court in 1954. In 1967, Marshall became the first African-American Supreme Court judge. He served on the court until 1993.

The Civil Rights Movement

The civil rights movement formed in the 1950s to push for equal treatment for all Americans. It used peaceful protests, such as the Montgomery bus boycott. This started in 1955 when Rosa Parks, an African-American woman, was **arrested** in Montgomery, Alabama, for refusing to give her seat on a bus to a white passenger. African Americans stopped riding buses there for over a year.

In 1964, the Civil Rights Act was passed. This act said that the rights given to citizens in the Constitution, such as the right to vote, must be upheld for all Americans.

Here is Rosa Parks (right) riding a Montgomery, Alabama, bus after the successful protest. African-American passengers could now sit anywhere on a bus and keep their seats. ▶

Martin Luther King Jr. was a leader in the civil rights movement. King was born on January 15, 1929, in Atlanta, Georgia. He helped lead the Montgomery bus boycott and protests in other cities.

Here is King standing beside a Montgomery, Alabama, bus after the boycott ended in 1956.

In 1963, King led the March on Washington. There, he gave a famous speech in which he shared his dream of living in a country where people are not judged "by the color of their skin but by the content of their character." Sadly, King died after being shot on April 4, 1968, in Memphis, Tennessee. Today, he is honored with a national holiday on the third Monday in January.

Thousands of people came to see King give his "I Have a Dream" speech during the March on Washington in 1963.

Respecting Everybody

Martin Luther King Jr. dreamed of a better America. We can all help that dream come true by respecting our fellow citizens.

If you hear a mean joke about African Americans, let people know it is not funny. If a bully picks on someone for looking different, tell the bully to stop. You can also tell an adult you trust about it. Show others that you believe that everyone deserves respect through your words and actions.

It is important to respect the things that make different groups of Americans special. It will help you understand that everyone deserves to be treated equally.

Glossary

amendment (uh-MEND-ment) An addition or a change to the Constitution.

ancestors (AN-ses-terz) Relatives who lived long ago.

arrested (uh-REST-ed) Stopped a person who is thought to have committed a crime.

citizens (SIH-tih-zenz) People who were born in or have a right to live in a country or other community.

Constitution (kon-stih-TOO-shun) The basic rules by which the United States is governed.

cyberbullies (SY-ber-bu-leez) People who do hurtful or threatening things to other people using the Internet.

Harlem Renaissance (HAR-lum REH-nuh-sons) A movement based in Harlem, the neighborhood in New York City, during the 1920s and 1930s of African American artists.

jazz (JAZ) A style of music that came from African American communities in the South in the early twentieth century.

lynched (LINCHD) Killed a person by mob action and without legal authority.

plantations (plan-TAY-shunz) Very large farms where crops are grown.

racism (RAY-sih-zum) The belief that one group or race of people, such as whites, is better than another group, such as blacks.

scholar (SKAH-ler) A person who has gone to school and who has much knowledge.

segregation (seh-grih-GAY-shun) The act of keeping people of one race, sex, or social class away from others.

Index

Websites

Due to the changing nature of Internet links, PowerKids Press has developed an online list of websites related to the subject of this book. This site is updated regularly. Please use this link to access the list:
www.powerkidslinks.com/sbn/african/